I0451873

Room for Company

PRAISE FOR *STORYSHARES*

"One of the brightest innovators and game-changers in the education industry."
– Forbes

"Your success in applying research-validated practices to promote literacy serves as a valuable model for other organizations seeking to create evidence-based literacy programs."

- Library of Congress

"We need powerful social and educational innovation, and Storyshares is breaking new ground. The organization addresses critical problems facing our students and teachers. I am excited about the strategies it brings to the collective work of making sure every student has an equal chance in life."
– Teach For America

"Around the world, this is one of the up-and-coming trailblazers changing the landscape of literacy and education."
- International Literacy Association

"It's the perfect idea. There's really nothing like this. I mean wow, this will be a wonderful experience for young people."   - Andrea Davis Pinkney, Executive Director, Scholastic

"Reading for meaning opens opportunities for a lifetime of learning. Providing emerging readers with engaging texts that are designed to offer both challenges and support for each individual will improve their lives for years to come. Storyshares is a wonderful start."
- David Rose, Co-founder of CAST & UDL

Room for Company

A.A. Gardner

STORYSHARES

Story Share, Inc.
New York. Boston. Philadelphia

Copyright © 2022 A. A. Gardner

All rights reserved.

Published in the United States by Story Share, Inc.

The characters and events in this book are fictitious. Any similarity to real persons, living or dead, is entirely coincidental.

Storyshares
Story Share, Inc.
24 N. Bryn Mawr Avenue #340
Bryn Mawr, PA 19010-3304
www.storyshares.org

Inspiring reading with a new kind of book.

Interest Level: Middle School
Grade Level Equivalent: 2.1

9798885979276

Book design by Storyshares

Printed in the United States of America

Storyshares Presents

1

"The roaders are bad luck," Aunt Delly said.

They came by the little town of Upper Dorne sometimes, in their colorful wagons. Spent a few evenings in the woods outside town. They were strange folk. Foreign folk. They didn't belong. Aunt Delly said they made milk go sour and turned well water to mud.

And they took away naughty children. Children who didn't behave. The roaders snatched them right up and stuck them in potato sacks. Aunt Delly said it was the smell. The roaders could smell naughty from ten miles away.

Whenever the roaders came to town, Noelle scrubbed herself in the wash basin until her skin was red. She sniffed under both armpits to make sure. Still, Aunt Delly said Noelle was the naughtiest girl she'd ever seen.

That night, Aunt Delly was pressing her bonnets and Uncle Jou was drinking his wine. Noelle was kneeling on walnut shells in the corner. Aunt Delly had punished her for talking back. The walnut shells cut into the skin of Noelle's knees. She hated when Aunt Delly made her sit in the corner like that, but Aunt Delly said it would teach her to be *good*.

Noelle was wondering how prickly shells and scraped knees were supposed to teach that when she heard the telltale noises outside. Horses brayed and wagon wheels *click-clacked*. Voices called out to each other in the distance.

She peeked out the window. Just outside the edge of town, wagons were pulling off the road into the shadow of the woods.

"Not again!" Aunt Delly left her blue bonnet unpressed. She went to the window. "I *told* the Mayor to set the dogs on them last time. They wouldn't have come back so soon if the dogs were out. Lazy good-for-nothings."

Uncle Jou mumbled something and took another swig of wine.

Noelle sniffed her shirt one last time, just to make sure. She couldn't smell any naughty.

"Go lock up the chicken coop," Aunt Delly told her. "With the good lock! And bring in the clothes off the line."

The roaders stole chickens, if they could get them. And shirts and pants drying on the clotheslines. The Mayor's wife said they stole the church collection money, once. Money for the poor! And they made the pond run dry and the chickens stop laying eggs.

"Jou, go get some extra buckets of water." Aunt Delly wrinkled her nose in disgust. "I don't want to use the well after *those people*. Jou, did you hear me? Oh, you're useless!"

Uncle Jou leaned back in his chair and grinned. "Delly, beautiful... beautiful girl." And he poured himself more wine.

Aunt Delly snapped her fingers at Noelle. "You go get the water."

Noelle was already putting on her shoes. She stopped, one hand on the left shoe. "I don't want to go to the well!"

"Don't talk back to me, naughty girl! Do you want me to tell the roaders to take you? Is that what you want? I'll toss you right out on the streets for them to take!"

Noelle didn't want that. She grabbed the water bucket from beside the door and ran to do Aunt Delly's bidding.

"Take two buckets!" Aunt Delly yelled behind her. But Noelle couldn't carry two buckets full of water. She pretended not to hear. She locked the chicken coop all in a hurry, then dashed out the front gate. She headed for the well.

2

Noelle's left shoe flew off while she ran. It never stayed on anymore. The ankle strap was old and frayed. But Aunt Delly said new shoes were only for *good children*.

The market bells tolled sunset. Noelle hurried on, shoe in her hand. She didn't want to be out at night!

Aunt Delly and Uncle Jou lived near the edge of town. Their neighbors were Old Pete the fisherman and Pierre who fixed shoes and Ramon who made glue. The Mayor and all of Aunt Delly's friends from church lived uptown. Aunt Delly always said it was Uncle Jou's fault that she didn't live uptown, too. But Noelle didn't mind living close to the woods.

Except for when the roaders were there.

She could see the orange light of their campfires in the woods. Old Pete said that roaders didn't stay put in their towns, like good folk should. They wandered. They cooked and ate and slept outside, and they carried everything they owned in their wagons. They carried away naughty children in their wagons, too.

Noelle reached the well at last. She hurried to drop the bucket down. The sooner she was done, the better!

The bucket slushed around the bottom of the well for a minute. Noelle decided it was full enough and began to crank it back up. It went fine about half of the way. Then, the chain snagged.

Froglegs!

Noelle tugged once, twice, but nothing happened. Of all the times for it to snag! Aunt Delly would peel her ears off her head if she came back without water.

She squinted to look where the rusted chain wrapped around the crank. It was all brown and dirty. No one ever oiled it. If only she could just find a way to unsnag it.

She put one knee on the edge of the well and climbed up to reach the chain. It was stuck somewhere in the middle, over the well shaft. She could see where a misshapen link had slipped under another. If she could just slip it back out...

Her hand grazed the chain link. She stretched the tips of her fingers as much as she could. The stuck bit moved.... a little. Then it moved a little more. And then...

Yes! Noelle grinned. *Success!*

She hopped back down from the edge of the well. She went back to the crank to get the bucket out.

Suddenly, arms grabbed her from behind.

Something dark and stuffy came down over her head and shoulders. A potato sack!

She barely had time to think about it before the sack swallowed her up completely. Noelle found herself hoisted up on foreign arms and carried away.

3

"Let go! Let go-o-o!"

Noelle kicked her legs. But the potato sack was sturdy. It didn't rip.

Her kidnappers carried her into the woods. The air smelled like wet earth and grass.

"Help! Somebody help!" she called. No one answered. "The mayor will send the dogs after you! The constable will... *oomph!*" The sack cloth got in her face. "He'll stick you in jail! Forever!"

There were giggles on the other side of the potato sack. Then someone made a hushing sound.

Noelle kicked her legs out again. There was an indignant, "Hey! Watch it!" Then another *shhh*, but too late. Noelle recognized the voice.

Little Pete! The fisherman's boy! She'd dunked him in the river just last week. He'd tried to rub stinging nettles on her face.

"You rotten little frogleg, Pete! Let me go right now! I'll tell on you!" Noelle thrashed. "And Nate, the butcher's boy! And Vlad! I know it's you! Put me down!"

An elbow dug painfully into her ribs. "Shut up, foundling" Vlad said. He was the mayor's son. He'd hated Noelle from the second she'd come to town. "We're taking you back where you belong."

"I'm not a foundling! Put me down!" Noelle yelled.

"If you're not a foundling, where's your parents, huh? Oh wait, they don't exist!" More laughter followed.

Noelle punched the air inside the potato sack.

"Momma says Delly found you on the road, like a stray cat. Cats don't live in houses, huh?"

"That's not true!" Noelle growled. "I'm gonna tell everyone on you! Let me go! He-e-e-elp!"

The nasty little boys laughed on. "You're a little foundling, and we're taking you back to your folk. Didn't you see? They came back for you! You can go live in a wagon like them, and sleep in a pile of horse dung."

The boys laughed more. But suddenly a new voice, an angry voice, rang out above Noelle's head. "What are you three doing? Get out of here! Put that down, now!"

The boys stumbled, frightened. They dropped Noelle. She screeched as she hit the ground. The new voice made an angry noise. The boys ran.

Served them right! Those nasty little frogs!

Noelle shoved the potato sack off her head. "I'll get you for this!" she screamed after the three boys. "I'll tell everyone you were gonna take me to the roaders! You're toast! You—"

She turned to thank her savior, and she froze. The man in front of her was short and skinny, with humped shoulders and a bald, pointy head. He looked surprised to see her, too.

"Devils take me!" he said. "I thought it was a dog in that sack!"

There was another man behind him. Tall like a bear, with a thick, black beard and bushy eyebrows. He scowled at Noelle like he wanted to eat her.

It was the roaders!

Vlad and his gang had brought her to the roaders!

4

Noelle ran for a long time, until she got turned around.

Night had fallen. Darkness made the woods look different. Tree branches loomed above like giant, grabby hands. Roots stretched like snakes on the ground. Everything was scratchy and grimy and *scary* and Noelle was lost... totally lost!

An owl hooted up in a tree, scaring her. Noelle flopped down to the ground and began to cry.

She didn't hear the footsteps. But suddenly a woman was standing over her, blocking the moonlight. She was tall, with long limbs and curly hair that stopped right above her shoulders.

"That's a lot of tears, little towngirl. Did you hurt yourself?" Her voice was low, raspy.

Noelle tried to hide in the bushes behind her.

"You're a mile out of town, do you know? But I can show you the way back."

Noelle threw a handful of wet leaves at her. "Leave me alone!"

The woman sighed. "I'm not going to hurt you. I'll take you back to your folks."

"You'll eat me!"

Giggles came from behind. The bushes rustled, and a girl and a boy popped up beside the woman. The girl was taller than Noelle, though not by much. The boy looked younger.

The woman put her hands on her hips. "You two are supposed to be washing the dinner plates."

"We wanted to know what the noise was all about!" The girl wore a big grin and dark hair in two long braids. "She thinks you want to eat her!"

"I heard. Now go back." The woman shooed them away. Then she held a hand down to Noelle. "Come on. I'll show you how to get back to your home. Get up, girl!" Her eyes narrowed. "Up. Or else I'm going to get that potato sack."

Noelle jumped to her feet. "No!"

The two kids giggled again. "I'm Rosebud," said the girl. "Are you really from town? What are you doing all alone in the woods? Oh, this is Remy."

The boy had been tugging on the hem of her shirt. He had floppy hair and a missing tooth. "I'm seven today!" He held up a short flute. "Look! Scapin gave it to me so I can play music!"

He blew into the flute. A strangled sort of noise came out, like the screech of an angry cat.

The woman waved a hand. "Go, you. And you, little towngirl, follow me." She led the way back through the woods.

Noelle stuck close to the girl and boy. "Did they steal you, too?" she whispered.

The woman made an angry noise.

But Rosebud laughed. "Who? Seren?"

"What did Seren steal?" Remy didn't know to keep his voice down.

"Button told me she took Grigor's horse, once. That's why he's still mad at her," Rosebud said.

The woman said a sharp word, and the boy fell silent. "Go back to camp. I'll be there soon. And stop listening to Button's tales."

"But—" Rosebud started to say.

The woman snapped her fingers. "Back, I said."

Rosebud sighed. She grabbed Remy's hand and they went down another path.

"And you, girl," the woman said. "Pick up the pace. We're close to your town."

Noelle didn't believe her. But when they reached a small clearing, she recognized the old, gnarled tree in the middle.

That's just a few minutes from town! Look, street lamps!

She could see the orange lights in the distance. She picked up the pace, eager to be out of the woods. The air smelled, strangely, like campfire...

Then the shouting began. Loud, angry voices, from the direction of town. The woman stopped.

What?

"Seren!" a voice shouted.

Noelle jumped.

The bear-man, the one with the big, black beard, came running from the trees. The bald one ran behind him.

"They've set a fire!"

The bear-man swore, ugly words that Noelle wasn't allowed to say. The smell of campfire grew stronger. It made Noelle's eyes itch.

"They set the dogs out, too! Go back! Back!"

Noelle stumbled over a branch and fell. The ground felt warm. There was more shouting and dogs barking. A dog jumped out of the bushes! Its teeth sank into the hem of her dress. Noelle screamed, and a hand grabbed her shoulder.

"Let go!" she meant to say. But smoke got in her mouth. She coughed.

The woods grew bright with firelight, and hot. Everything began to move too fast. Everyone was running. People were shouting. Noelle's heart beat so fast she thought it might jump out of her chest.

5

Noelle woke up on a lumpy bed. The ceiling was blue.

Wait... that wasn't a ceiling.

She was looking up at a piece of blue canvas.

Blue canvas! Noelle jumped up. *The roader's wagons were blue!*

They'd stolen her after all!

The wagon was moving. Noelle scrambled back. But before she could jump out, a hand moved the canvas cover at the front. A long face with hazel eyes peered back at Noelle. The woman from the woods!

"Good morning."

Noelle let out a frightened squeak.

The woman turned to say something to the person on her left. There was a click of a tongue and a hoarse "Ho!" The wagon stopped.

Noelle jumped out before they could stop her.

She landed on her knees on the dusty road. There was nothing around except trees and shrubs and dry grass. The road snaked over low hills as far as Noelle could see. It looked empty. No house or town in sight.

She started to run, but after two steps a hand closed around her arm.

"Wait."

"Let go!"

The woman held on. "There are animals around here. Robbers, too. It's dangerous to run."

"Help!"

But no one answered.

"You're safe with us," said the woman. "I'm Seren. We met last night."

"You said you were taking me back!"

"Your townsfolk set fires in the woods. It cut into our path, do you remember? And they set dogs loose."

Noelle remembered. She could still taste smoke on her tongue. She remembered running from the dogs, too. Old Pete's hounds and the Mayor's hunting dogs.

"It wasn't my fault they let the dogs out! I didn't tell them to!"

"I know."

"Then let me go! Please! I'll— I'll pay you! Do you want money?"

Noelle didn't have any money. But that was a problem she'd consider after.

Seren sighed. "We're thirty miles away by now, towngirl."

"What?"

"The fire spread. We had to get out of the area." Seren shook her head. "It wasn't safe to leave you out there. But I didn't realize we'd keep the wagons going through the night. There was... a misunderstanding."

Noelle stared. *Thirty miles? That was hours and hours and hours!*

"I can't get the company to turn around for you, but—"

"Eh! Lady Ona!" A man was shouting from the wagon ahead. "Why'd you stop?"

There were five or six wagons in front of them, Noelle noticed. They stretched out on the road like ants on a picnic blanket.

"Why do you think?" shouted a sour voice from the front of the wagon. Then a sour face looked back on the road. It was an old woman, with a pointy nose and large spectacles. "Are you done with the townie, girl? Or do you want to hold up the whole company again?"

Seren waved to the man ahead, "Keep going!" She turned back to Noelle. "We'll be in Rou-by-the-Sea in only a couple of days. We'll write your parents. They can come get you there."

Noelle was still staring. "I don't have parents anymore," she wanted to say. But her voice wasn't working yet.

Vlad, the mayor's nephew, was right. Kids who didn't have parents ended up with the roaders.

"Eh!" The old woman looked back again. "What's taking so long? We're falling behind!"

"We're coming." Seren gave Noelle a long look. "Things are what they are, little towngirl. We'll have to make the best of them. Come on." She brought Noelle to the front of the wagon. "You can sit up by Lady Ona if you want. See the road."

Noelle *didn't* want. But there was nowhere to run. No one to help her.

Lady Ona clicked her tongue and the wagon began to move again.

6

The wagons stopped around noon for a break. Immediately, Rosebud and Remy ran over. Noelle didn't admit it, but she was glad to see them.

Remy pulled her into the shade of a tree, and Rosebud began to ask her questions.

"Is it true the townsfolk threw you out?"

"What? No!" Noelle thought of Vlad and the other boys. "It was just a stupid prank!"

"Is it true they put you in a potato sack?" asked Remy.

"We saw them get you, at the well. Why did you climb into the well?"

"I wasn't! The chain was snagged. I had to fix it. That's why I didn't see those nasty boys."

Rosebud spit on the ground. "If they tried to put me in a sack, I'd pluck their eyes out!"

"I will when I'm back!" Noelle said. Then she remembered how far she was, and who she was with. The roaders hadn't eaten her yet, but it was lunch time.

She pulled back. "If they didn't steal you, how did you get here?"

Remy gave Rosebud a confused look. The girl shook her head, braids flying to and fro. "Townies are all weird like that. How do you *think* we got here? How did you get to *your* family?"

Noelle crossed her arms. "My parents died, so I had to go live with Aunt Delly and Uncle Jou."

Rosebud frowned. She looked at Noelle like she didn't believe her. "You got no parents?"

"I'm not a foundling!" Noelle shouted.

"Rosebud's parents had to go, too." Remy bit his lips, like he wasn't sure he was allowed to talk about it. When Rosebud didn't stop him, he went on. "They used to live on a boat!"

"A ship," Rosebud corrected. "Anyway, that's how I got here. Remy's Pere's son." She pointed to the white-haired man who drove the first wagon. "He's the leader of the company. That's his wife, Mila."

"My momma," said Remy.

"I ride with Violette and Grigor." Rosebud pointed to the third wagon. "They took me in after... you know. But no one stole us!" She scowled, but her eyes looked sad. Then she started to point to other wagons, and Noelle understood that she didn't want to talk about parents anymore.

"That's Bran, Violette's brother. He doesn't talk, but he's real good at drawing. The second wagon is Jove's. The tall boy is her son, Button. Scapin is Jove's brother." Rosebud pointed to the bald man. "He's a carpenter. He makes the sets and props out of wood."

"He made my flute!" Remy blew into the flute again.

"What sets?" Noelle asked.

"The stage sets." Rosebud gave Noelle a funny look. "You ride in Lady Ona's cart... didn't you see all the wooden swords and cutouts and things?"

Noelle had seen them. She just didn't know what they were.

"Pere's company is a traveling theater. Actors." Rosebud rolled her eyes at Noelle's confusion. "Didn't you ever hear of theater?"

"I did! But I thought..." Noelle scratched her head. She hadn't wondered what the roaders did. Aunt Delly said they wandered because they had nothing better to do. "So you're an actor?"

Rosebud shrugged. "Only if Pere puts on a play that needs a lot of extra folk around on the stage. I don't like it. And Remy's too young."

"*I* like it!" Remy grinned. "Pere lets me do all the kid roles. When I grow up, I'll get to do the knight roles! Rosebud can be my sweet lady."

Rosebud flicked his nose with her fingers. "I'm gonna learn how to make costumes from Jove! I don't like being on stage."

Remy turned on Noelle. "Then *you* can be my sweet lady! Do you like to be on stage?"

"What? I've never been on stage! And I'm not staying here!" She looked from Remy to Rosebud. "Is this why they stole me? For theater?"

"Again with that!" Rosebud scowled. "Seren didn't force you to run from that fire, you know!"

"But I was scared! I wanted to run back to town, not join a traveling theater!"

"You don't have to be on stage." Remy patted her knee. "Some company folk do other things! Like Lady Ona, who makes sure the wagons run right. Tippi and

Emmeline just pick plants and sell them. Jove makes costumes, Seren—"

"I don't want to do any of that!" Noelle shot up to her feet. "I want to go back to town!"

"Well, we're not!" said Rosebud. "Your stupid townies tried to set us on fire! And they chased us off with dogs!

"Just because they thought you were gonna steal things!"

"That's because they're stupid!"

"Stop yelling!" Remy yelled.

An older woman near them shouted, "Meal's ready!"

Rosebud and Remy jumped to their feet. Noelle hung back.

"Aren't you hungry?" asked Remy.

Rosebud scoffed. "She doesn't want to eat with us. She thinks she's too good."

Before Noelle could reply, Seren walked over. "Come along. Guests eat with their hosts."

"I'm not your guest, you stole me!"

"She didn't!" Rosebud glared, but Seren said, "That's enough. Go on, get to the table. You too, Noelle."

Noelle shuffled along. They'd probably drag her to the table, if she didn't. She just hoped she wasn't the main course!

Rosebud hissed angrily as they walked, "You know, Pere got mad at Seren for bringing you along. He says townsfolk are nothing but trouble." She scowled. "And I think he's right! Trouble, and stupid!"

And with that, she marched on ahead, turning her back on Noelle.

7

Noelle felt like a juicy worm in a room full of hungry birds.

Everyone was staring at her. Two dozen roaders, young and old, men and women. Most didn't look happy to see her.

They'd all gathered around a low, wooden table on the grass. Remy had gone to sit next to his parents.

Rosebud had snuck behind the bear-man, Grigor. She was still scowling.

"This is Noelle," Seren told everyone. "With Pere's permission, she'll be our guest until Rou-by-the-Sea."

Pere, the man with white hair and broad shoulders, sighed. He didn't look happy, either.

"Townsfolk have no business being here," Grigor grumbled.

Seren put her hands on her hips and scowled at him. Whispers broke out.

But the younger woman next to Pere held up her hands. "Please. Seren has the right to bring a guest. And we always have room for company. Noelle is welcome."

Seren smiled. "Thank you, Mila."

Remy grinned behind his mother. Pere made a grumpy sort of noise. "All right. Just keep her out of the way." He shook his head. "Lady Ona, make sure the wheels are well oiled. I want to get to Rou-by-the-Sea quickly."

The old woman cackled. Then Pere waved a hand toward the big pot of stew on the table. "God bless," he said. And everyone began to serve themselves.

Noelle hung back. When Seren presented her with a tin bowl full of stew, she sniffed it, suspicious. "What's in it?"

"A child from the last village." Seren rolled her eyes. "It's rabbit, girl. Just eat it. It'll be a long two days if you go hungry."

Noelle *was* hungry. But her stomach hurt from being scared. She pushed the bowl away. "Why can't we turn around to Upper Dorne?"

"Your stupid townies, that's why!" Rosebud had circled around the table. "We didn't even do anything to them!"

"It's 'cause they're scared." Remy had walked over with his bowl. "Momma says that's why townies are so mean."

"That's not true!"

"It is!" said Rosebud. "We never met a nice townie!"

"Well I never met a nice roader!"

"Stop calling us that!"

"You turn the milk sour and make the fish die! And you stole me!"

"What?" said Remy.

"We didn't steal you!"

"Stop yelling." Seren thumped Rosebud on the shoulder with her spoon. "You're disturbing everyone's meal. And you..." Her amber eyes turned on Noelle. "Those are ugly things you keep saying."

"But—"

"What you believe is your business. But the words we say have power. If you can't keep your words civil, then perhaps you should sit quietly."

Rosebud crossed her arms, all smug. "I see why your townie friends put you in that potato sack. I'd want to get rid of you, too."

"Rosebud," Seren warned.

Noelle gritted her teeth. "At least I don't have to sleep with horses!"

"What's wrong with the horses?" Remy was looking from Noelle to Rosebud. "Who makes the fish die?"

"No one. Rosebud, go help Jove get water." Seren snapped her fingers. *"Now,* please. Remy, your mother wants you."

"I don't see her calling."

"I did. Go see what she wants." She waved both of them away. Then she turned to Noelle.

Noelle's hands went to cover her ears. Just in case Seren wanted to tug on them. "She started it!"

"It's not Rosebud and Remy's fault that you're here when you don't want to be."

"No," said Noelle.

It was Seren's fault. Hers and the bald man's, Scapin, who'd hauled her through the woods to the wagons. It was *their* fault.

Seren went to help Violette's brother cut bread. He thanked her with noises that didn't sound like words. But

Seren seemed to get it. Others did, too. They talked to the tall older boy, even if he didn't talk back. He didn't sit alone. No one did. Not Bran, not Lady Ona, who looked like a mean old witch. Not even Grigor, who scowled all the time.

Noelle went to sit by one of the trees. No one stopped her. She sat down and hugged her knees to her chest. Something inside her felt hollow.

8

Noelle rode in the back of Lady Ona's wagon. She didn't care to see the road. No one cared to see her. She was mad, and scared, and very, very hungry.

There was a half-eaten loaf of bread in the wagon, and a handful of berries in a wooden bowl. Noelle picked at the fruit. After a little while, she nibbled at the bread, too. She was no better than the roaders, taking food that wasn't hers. But her stomach was rumbling.

Besides, there was no more punishment to suffer for being naughty. The roaders already had her.

At night, they pulled over to the side of the road again. They found cover in a small clump of trees. After a little while, Seren came to get Noelle. "Dinner," she said. "Guests eat with their hosts."

"I'm not your guest," mumbled Noelle. She was starving, but she felt contrary.

Seren motioned for her to come along, anyway. Hunger won over. Noelle went.

Things went much the same as lunch. She sat by a tree with a bowl of stew. People shot her crooked looks now and then. But no one said anything. No one tried to eat her.

After a while, Remy sneaked away from his mother. "I didn't mean to make you sad, earlier. When I said townies are scared." He looked nervous. "I didn't know that wasn't *civil.*"

Noelle shrugged.

"Momma says we don't steal anyone. I asked her. And we don't make fish die, either. Or milk go bad."

He was too little to know better. "She'll be mad you're talking to me."

Remy glanced back. "She said townies always look for folk to blame for bad stuff. But I told her you were nice. And she says I'm allowed to play with you if I want to."

Noelle shrugged. She didn't mind him talking to her. "Okay."

"And she said *for sure* no one steals children! So you don't have to be scared, okay?" He pointed to Noelle's empty bowl. "You want more dinner? I'll get you more!"

He'd already picked up the bowl before Noelle could answer. But she was still hungry, so she let him go. He was back in a minute.

"I spilled some, sorry. Oh! I lost the spoon!" he said.

"That's okay." Aunt Delly wasn't there to yell at Noelle for slurping straight out of the bowl. "Thanks."

While she sipped the warm stew, she looked around the camp for Rosebud. The girl was helping tie the horses to a couple of trees. Their eyes met for a second. Then Rosebud scowled and went back to the horses. Noelle went back to her stew.

"I'm gonna play my music after we eat! Wanna hear?" Remy asked.

Remy tried his flute again. It still sounded like a sad cat. But one of the men joined in, with an instrument made out of little pipes. Real music came out when he played. A few of the others began to sing. The summer night was warm and the fire was cozy.

Before she knew it, Noelle found a hand shaking her shoulder.

"You'll be more comfortable lying down."

Noelle was confused. "What?" The music hadn't stopped, but Remy was gone. She yawned.

"Come on." Seren helped her up. Noelle didn't remember sitting against a tree. "You can sleep in the wagon, if you don't mind Lady Ona's snoring."

Noelle yawned again. "Do I have to sleep with the horses, too?"

"You're talking nonsense, girl." Seren guided her into the wagon, and Noelle was content to find a soft surface to lie on, and a blanket to huddle under.

"Maybe I'm dreaming," she decided.

"Maybe," said Seren. "Go to sleep. You'll be back home soon."

Noelle was too tired to explain to her that Aunt Delly and Uncle Jou's house wasn't her home. She rolled over instead, and she was asleep again in less than a minute.

9

The rain made the wagons move slowly. Big, heavy drops fell against the blue cover. *Plop. Plop.* Everything was gray and glum.

"Is the rain gonna make you miss the summer festival?" Noelle asked. She thought Seren should feel equally glum, at least.

The Rou-by-the-Sea festival was a big affair. Weeks of selling and buying and singing and eating. People came from all over. Noelle's parents had gone once, when she was very young. She remembered eating lots of fried fish and sugar fruit. Momma laughing as they danced.

"We'll be there by tomorrow. Plenty of time to enjoy the festival."

"Aunt Delly says festivals are for folks with nothing better to do," Noelle said. She didn't know why she wanted to get a rise out of Seren.

But Seren didn't get mad. "I'm sure we'll find things to do once we're there."

"Like what?" Noelle glanced at the wooden props in the back. "A play?"

"That," said Seren, "and getting supplies, and meeting old friends. Many folk travel to Rou-by-the-Sea in summer. And our craftsmen sell their wares there, too."

"You have craftsmen?"

"Scapin makes chairs and flutes. Jove makes scarves to sell. Emmeline and Tippi spent the last month extracting flower oils and pressing herbs."

"And people buy from you?"

Seren's lips pressed together.

"I— I mean—"

"I know what you mean."

"Just because... I mean, people say roaders..." Noelle bit her lips. "Uh, you people..."

"Company folk," said Seren. "That's a civil word to call us."

"Company folk." Noelle tried it out. It sounded weird. "Because you're a theater company?"

"It just means a group of people who travel together. Company folk come from many different places, and they travel for different reasons. Some, like Pere, go around doing the thing they love. Others travel for other kinds of work, or because they prefer to be on the road. Others because they don't have a choice."

Like me, Noelle wanted to say. But for some reason she was done wanting to make Seren mad. "So it's the other company folk who make milk sour and steal naughty children?"

Seren closed her eyes and let out a slow breath.

Lady Ona glanced over. "Grigor told you to toss her on the road when we left those woods."

Seren's cheeks reddened.

"I'm sorry!" Noelle felt bad, but she wasn't sure why.

Seren turned to her. "What are you sorry for?"

Noelle didn't know. She just knew there was a knot in her stomach that didn't feel good.

"Ho." Lady Ona stopped the cart. "You'll catch your death in this rain, boy."

Remy ran up to the side of the wagon. "Pere said I could ride with you and Seren and Noelle!" He grinned up at them, with his missing tooth. "And I'm not wet! Jove made me a rain coat!"

"Come up faster." Seren reached a hand down. Remy climbed up into her lap, and she shifted him over to the back of the wagon. "There."

"Pere said I could make *your* ears hurt with questions," said Remy. "But I... Oh, look, there's Rosebud! I asked Grigor and Violette if she can come."

"No one asked *me* if I wanted a party," grumbled Lady Ona. "This is my wagon." But she didn't turn Rosebud away.

Noelle was wary.

Rosebud still wasn't looking all that friendly. "I only came cause Remy asked me," she said, as soon as she was on. Then she pulled something from under her rain cloak. "Bran wanted you to have this. I don't know *why*. You didn't even talk to him."

She handed Noelle a large piece of thick paper. Her rain cloak had protected it from the rain.

It was a drawing, in charcoal and ink. It showed a large tree, with a wagon beside it. A girl sat against the tree, knees to her chest. A bowl rested on the ground beside her.

The girl was Noelle. She recognized her pigtails and the frilly dress. Like her, the girl wore only socks. But the girl's expression was sad. She was looking up ahead, like she wanted something very badly but she couldn't have it.

"Looks just like you!" Remy was looking over her shoulder. "Isn't Bran great? He draws me forest animals all the time."

Noelle bit her lips. She couldn't take her eyes off the face of the girl in the drawing.

"Don't you like it?" Remy sounded worried.

Rosebud was beginning to scowl again.

"No. I mean yes, I do! It's... it's really good. Bran is great at drawing." She looked at Rosebud. "Can I keep it?"

The girl rolled her eyes. "You don't think he made it for me, do you? It's yours."

"Thanks." On impulse, Noelle added, "Maybe he could draw me one of the two of you, too."

Rosebud looked surprised. Remy looked delighted.

"Yeah!" Remy said.

"Maybe if you ask him," said Rosebud.

"I will," Noelle said.

Rosebud's lips twitched in a small smile. Noelle smiled back.

10

"Look!" Remy shouted. "We can throw darts at water balloons! There's a lady on big, wooden sticks! I want to see the ponies! Pere said there's ponies! Let's get fried fish first! I want to go swim in the sea!"

Seren interrupted with a clap of her hands. "Rosebud, hold Remy's hand and stay close to Bran and Violette. We'll get fried fish later. Noelle and I have to go write to her family."

"We'll go too! We never saw a post office!"

Seren took Noelle, Remy and Rosebud onto the busy streets of Rou-by-the-Sea. There were hundreds of people there for the summer festival. Everything was loud and colorful.

They wrote to Aunt Delly and Uncle Jou and sent the letter on the fastest route. But it would be at least two days before they could come get Noelle. She had time to enjoy the festival.

"Did you ever eat sugar fruit?" Rosebud asked Remy.

Remy had not. He begged for some until Seren gave in. By the afternoon, they'd eaten more sugar pears and fried fish than they could stomach.

They saw dozens of vendors, too. Rosebud got two ribbons for her braids, in bright blue silk. Seren bought Remy a small bird whistle. She got Noelle a new pair of shoes.

The company had settled on the beach. Pere set up a little theater with the sets and props from Lady Ona's wagon. Scapin's chairs were for the audience to sit on.

Jove's son, Button, played the knight. He entertained Remy with his practice with the wooden sword.

Everyone helped set things up. Remy and Noelle arranged chairs. Rosebud, being older, was trusted with arranging lamps on the stage. Bran was painting yellow flowers on one of the props. Grigor and Scapin went around town announcing the upcoming performance.

By evening, every chair was full. Some people were standing, too. One of the company folk walked among them with a wooden bowl for coins.

Noelle had never seen a play. She knew the people on stage, but in their bright costumes they looked different. They talked differently, too. Pere was louder, Violette shrill. Lenore, who always laughed at the dinner table, acted stern. Scapin pretended to be afraid of Button. They seemed like different people altogether.

Then there was the music. Two company folk played on each side of the stage. The music boomed when there was a fight on the stage. It turned soft for a lover's meeting.

Noelle was spellbound.

At the end, the company folk took a deep bow. The audience cheered and stamped their feet.

Noelle couldn't stop talking about the play for the rest of the night. She asked Seren about every single scene. She remembered every time someone had done something funny, or something sad.

Rosebud laughed and told Noelle she'd end up on a stage, after all. Pere winked at her.

She wished the night would never end.

The next days were much the same. In daytime, they helped Scapin and Jove and the others set up stands to sell their wares. Sometimes they went around with Button or Violette, buying supplies. Seren made Noelle send a few more letters, in case one got lost. In the evenings, the company set up the same play. Noelle never got tired of watching.

They celebrated after each performance. There was music and warm food. Scapin gave Noelle a little flute of her own. Remy offered to teach her to play. They fell asleep listening to singing and the sound of waves every night, and the next day everything started up again.

It was the best time Noelle could ever remember.

She didn't notice the days passing. She didn't realize they'd been there a week, with no response from Aunt Delly and Uncle Jou.

They didn't come get her. They didn't write back. Seren checked every day. Soon the festival was near its end, and there had been no sign from them.

The last day, Noelle skipped the preparation for the play to go meet the stagecoach. It was the third one that had come by way of Upper Dorne. Neither Aunt Delly nor Uncle Jou was on it.

She understood.

They weren't coming.

11

"The company's going to turn around."

Noelle put down her breakfast plate. "What?"

Seren sat cross-legged on the sand, on their empty corner of the beach. The sun had reddened her nose and cheeks. No one in Pere's company wore bonnets.

"We've agreed. We'll go back east instead of north, like we intended. Go to the lower provinces. We'll stop by Upper Dorne and return you to your family."

"But... I don't want to go back."

Noelle hadn't really thought about it. Aunt Delly and Uncle Jou hadn't come for her. That was just how it was. She didn't feel as sad as that girl in Bran's drawing.

Until Seren mentioned going back.

Seren looked surprised by her answer. "I'm sure there's a reason your relatives didn't respond. They're probably out looking for you. Worried..."

"Aunt Delly wouldn't look for me. Uncle Jou probably doesn't even know I'm gone! They don't really like me very much." Noelle thought for a moment. "I don't like them, either."

Seren sighed. "We don't always like our family. But—"

"Aunt Delly and Uncle Jou aren't *family* family. Not like you are to Rosebud and Remy and Pere and everyone. They just took me in so Aunt Delly's friends at church wouldn't gossip."

"Noelle!"

"I want to stay with your company!" Noelle glanced around. The others were starting to pack the wagons. "I'll be helpful! I'll brush the horses. I'll... I'll help set up the plays. I'll work for my keep. I'll start right now!" She jumped to her feet, ready to help.

But Seren held her back. "Little towngirl." She hadn't called Noelle that in days. "I'm so glad for your change of heart. Everyone's seen it. But Pere's company isn't your home. You'd feel the difference very soon."

"No, I wouldn't!" Noelle's voice broke. "Rosebud and Remy want me to stay! Bran wants me to stay. Even Lady Ona wouldn't mind, I bet. Why don't you want me to stay? What did I do?"

Seren bit her lips. "Noelle. This isn't your place. You have a home, and people who love you."

"They don't!" Noelle threw her hands up, "Didn't you see? They didn't come for me! They don't care! I might as well stay here!"

She knew she'd said something wrong when Seren twitched. But she didn't know what. "I'm sorry!"

Seren sighed. "What for?"

"Because you're mad. Please, Seren. Please let me stay. I know Pere will listen if you ask him to... Everyone here likes me, at least a little, please..."

Seren looked away. Her voice was sad. "Being mad at your family isn't a good reason to want to stay, Noelle. It's not fair to you, or to them, or to us." She met Noelle's eyes. "You belong with your own family."

"I'm not mad! They don't want me! And I don't want them!"

Seren gave her a look full of pity. "I know the people we love most can hurt us most, sometimes. But running away doesn't heal those hurts. Trust me. Home isn't a place you can run from." She smiled. "But I promise you, family finds a way to fix hurt feelings together. That's what family is. There's always something better waiting past the hurt."

Noelle shook her head. "Not with Aunt Delly and Uncle Jou. But I thought *you* wanted me, at least! I thought you liked me!" Her voice broke again. "You're the one who brought me here!"

"You know how that happened. Noelle, please." Seren clasped her hands together. "Please don't think we're not your friends. Everyone in the company has grown fond of you."

"But not enough to want me to be one of you!" Noelle's voice was bitter.

Seren closed her eyes. "You're not ours to want." When she blinked, her eyes were wet. "We don't steal other people's children."

"But it's not stealing if I want to stay!"

"I doubt your aunt and uncle would see it that way. No, I'm sorry, Noelle. You're not going to change my mind. Please." She let out a long breath, and stood up. "Please, go pack up your things. We're leaving right after breakfast. If the weather holds, we'll be in Upper Dorne by tomorrow night."

12

The way back was silent. Noelle didn't speak to Seren, not a word. Rosebud sat with her in the back of the wagon. She didn't speak to Seren, either. Remy cried. But even his tears didn't change Seren's mind. She always gave him everything, but not this time.

Noelle spotted the church steeple of Upper Dorne in early afternoon. Within an hour, they were on the far side of the woods. The air still smelled like smoke, a little.

You could see a few half-burned trees from the road. Pere halted the wagons about a mile out of town.

"Here, take these." Rosebud took off her hair ribbons and put them in Noelle's hands. "So you have something to remember me by."

Noelle looked down at the strips of blue silk. "Like I need a reminder." They laughed together through the tears. "I don't have anything to give you," Noelle said sadly. All she had were gifts from the company. "Do you want my shoes?"

Rosebud made a noise between a laugh and a hiccup. "Your shoes don't fit me."

"Then... here." Noelle gave her back one of the ribbons. "We'll each take one. Then we'll know the other has the pair."

They hugged so tight, Noelle thought she heard bones crack. She hugged Remy, too, and Bran, and Violette and Jove and Scapin and even Lady Ona.

Seren was waiting to walk her back to town, but Noelle turned away. She heard Seren say her name. But Noelle didnt want to talk to her. She reached for Scapin's hand, instead.

"Little girl," he said.

Noelle just scowled. "Do you want to take me back, or no? I can walk alone!"

Scapin looked over his shoulder, back to Seren. Then he sighed. "All right. Let's go."

"We love you," Remy cried from behind. Violette had wrapped her arms around him.

"Don't forget about us!" said Rosebud.

Noelle tucked her chin into her chest. *Never,* she wanted to say. But the words were stuck in her throat.

Scapin walked her slowly until the end of Main Street. He patted her shoulder, then she stepped away. "Don't look so glum. We're travelers. We'll come visit."

Noelle looked away. "Thanks."

"Good luck," said Scapin. And then he was gone. He vanished back into the woods. Noelle began to drag her new shoes along the dusty street.

13

Aunt Delly looked shocked to see Noelle. She stood frozen for a moment, hand on the doorknob. Then she recovered. "You! What are... How did... Get in here!" She pulled Noelle inside. "The neighbors will see!"

"I got caught in that forest fire. The company folk took me with them to Rou-by-the-Sea. Didn't you get my letters?"

Aunt Delly stared. "No," she said at last. But Noelle could tell she was lying.

Uncle Jou sat in his usual chair inside, his favorite wine mug in front of him. "Girl!" He waved the mug in Noelle's direction when she came in. "Made it back, hm? Told you, Delly."

"Shut up." Aunt Delly was still frowning. Like she hadn't decided yet how to react. "Shame on you! Running from home!"

"I didn't!"

"Don't lie!" Aunt Delly tugged on Noelle's ponytail. "Naughty girl!"

For a moment, Noelle had the familiar tug of fear. *Naughty children got taken away!* And then the fear became something else, in the hollow pit of her stomach. Anger. Sadness. Shame. And something stranger, too. A sort of longing Noelle didn't understand. The sort that Bran had put in the eyes of the girl in his drawing.

She still had the bag with all their gifts. She reached in and pulled out the second drawing Bran had done. It showed her and Remy and Rosebud, by Lady Ona's cart.

The girl with Noelle's face didn't look sad and alone in this drawing.

She looked at home.

Tears sprung from Noelle's eyes.

"What's the matter with you?" Aunt Delly scowled. "What's that?"

What had Seren said? That there was something better past the hurt? Noelle tried to find it.

"Do you want me here, Aunt Delly? Why didn't you come after me?"

"What? Jou! Do you hear this?"

"I sent you letters. Why didn't you come? Do you want me, even a little? Do you, Uncle Jou?"

Uncle Jou put down the wine jug. "Not so loud, girl. Go away and be quiet."

"You hear her, Jou? After all we did. Could've left you on the streets, naughty girl! Who'd have taken care of you? The roaders? You want to sleep with horses and steal like a thief?"

Noelle gritted her teeth. *The hurts don't heal running away*, she reminded herself. Family worked on the anger.

"Do either of you *want* me here with you? Do you want us to be a family?"

Aunt Delly stared at her like she'd never seen her before. "Get those filthy clothes off and go wash. I could smell you from a mile out. And quit it with the stupid questions."

Noelle looked away.

"And stop crying. God, you're a grown girl, not a toddler. What's the matter with you?"

Noelle looked at Bran's second drawing again. Remy was playing the flute. Rosebud had a pen in her hand. And Noelle, the Noelle on the paper, was smiling.

Suddenly, she realized what it was that she said that made Seren unhappy.

"Shame," Aunt Delly muttered. "Shame of the neighborhood, we were. Child in our household running away from home. Running with the roaders..."

"This isn't my home," Noelle said. "And that's not a nice word to call them."

Aunt Delly made an angry noise. Her hand gripped Noelle's ear. Noelle had forgotten to cover her ears. But she didn't ask Aunt Delly for forgiveness. She didn't say she was sorry.

Seren was wrong about Aunt Delly and Uncle Jou. They didn't want to be a family. And Seren was wrong about Noelle, too. She thought Noelle wanted to stay because she had nowhere better to go. She thought Noelle wanted to stay because she was mad at her relatives.

Seren was wrong about everything!

But only because Noelle herself hadn't known what she wanted.

"Ow!" She pulled away from Aunt Delly, before Aunt Delly could peel her ear off. "I'm going to wash up."

She ran over to the kitchen where the wash basin was. The same one she'd used to scrub the naughty smell off.

The tears were still falling. But Noelle didn't mind so much, now. She thought she had an idea of what she wanted.

She splashed cold water on her face. In the living room, Aunt Delly was muttering about "shame" and "neighbors" and "naughty."

Seren was right about one thing. You *couldn't* run away from home. Home wasn't a place you ran from. It was a place you ran *to*. Or sometimes, Noelle supposed, home was the people you ran to. Even if you were mad at them.

It was okay to be sad and mad. Sometimes that meant something better was waiting after the hurt.

Noelle hoped that Seren was right about that, too.

About The Author

A.A. Gardner is the author of Room for Company, a gripping tale for all ages about the true definition of family. Her book received an honorable mention from Storyshares's panel of judges following their 2021 Story of the Year contest.

About The Publisher

Story Shares is a nonprofit focused on supporting the millions of teens and adults who struggle with reading by creating a new shelf in the library specifically for them. The ever-growing collection features content that is compelling and culturally relevant for teens and adults, yet still readable at a range of lower reading levels.

Story Shares generates content by engaging deeply with writers, bringing together a community to create this new kind of book. With more intriguing and approachable stories to choose from, the teens and adults who have fallen behind are improving their skills and beginning to discover the joy of reading. For more information, visit storyshares.org.

Easy to Read. Hard to Put Down.

www.ingramcontent.com/pod-product-compliance
Lightning Source LLC
Chambersburg PA
CBHW051313170626
46809CB00004B/1881